He sang for his friends, whether asked to **or not,**
and here's the funniest thing:
whatever they said went
into his head as . . .

"That was
a-ma-zing!"

Every night, he had the same **dream** —

fame would knock on his door!

But **every day,** he'd wake to find

things as they were before.

Then one day,
he saw a **sign.**
It said:
"COME TO OUR AUDITIONS!"

"I've got the
fox factor!"
Fabio thought.
"I'll win and fulfill
my **ambitions."**

TALENT SHOW
COME TO OUR AUDITIONS!
RECORDED LIVE!
SATURDAY, 4AM, FOXTON ALLEY

Fabio stood still while the judges looked stern. They asked,

"What song will you do?"

He said,

"Wash your Socks, Stinky Fox."

That created a

hullabaloo!

The audience was lost for words – his performance was so **bizarre!**

A **million** views made Fabio Fox

an overnight

Internet

star!

Finally **famous,** Fabio's life changed in fabulous ways.
Glitz and glamour **24/7,** this was a typical day:

Wake up and have
a relaxing bubble bath

Gourmet breakfast of
French toast squares
on sticks

Luxury spa session,
including brush,
tint, and curl

Photo shoot for a fancy magazine

Be chased by paparazzi while just trying to lead a normal life

Elegant dinner of fried eggs shaped like stars

And to make sure he always arrived on time (or was it just to be seen?), with 16 seats and a Jacuzzi, he hired a **stretch limousine!**

Fabio's life soon **became** all he **dreamt** it would be.

He landed a recording contract – **"Stinky Fox"** was out on **CD!**

At a party in his **new**
penthouse,
Fabio took to the **floor,**
surrounded by his
fancy **new friends** –
his old ones were
stopped at the door.

This should have been
Fabio's moment –
a superstar truly born.
But remember, Fabio **could not sing** –
he **honked** like an old **foghorn.**

Watching Fabio **dance** on stage
would **fill** your heart with **glee.**
But who would buy his music?
Every note hit was **off-key!**

The DJs said,

"We can't play that!

We're sorry if this

sounds **rude."**

"But it'll give our

listeners an **earache,**

and none of us

wants to be **sued!"**

Stinky Fox was the **Flop of the Year**;
Fabio's fame was at an **end.**
He threw a party to **cheer** himself up
and invited his **VIP** friends.

But everyone was **too busy –**
no one could make the trip.
So Fabio had a party for **one,**
alone with his chip-'n'-dip.

FABIO

They took away Fabio's **limo** and the **keys** to his penthouse pad.

This was now Fabio's **typical** day –
gray and a little bit sad:

But, though he
didn't know it,
all was far from lost.
His story took
another twist,
now he'd learned what
fame had **cost . . .**

Walking through the streets one night,

Fabio heard a **familiar sound.**

He followed the noise through the alleys,

and **look** who he finally found!

His old friends were dancing to **"Stinky Fox"** –

what a **terrible** din!

"We made up this dance to remember you.

We found your CD **in a bin!**"

Fabio saw he'd been a fool.
"I won **fame** but lost my **friends** –
I forgot what really mattered.
How can I make **amends?**"

His **friends** said they would have to think,
but it didn't take them long:
they asked Fabio Fox to join them
in **remaking** his terrible song.

The friends all worked **together**, each doing what they did **best**.

The song now sounded much **better**,
but who could have guessed the rest?

Their group became a worldwide smash:

Fabio's Famous Crew!